A
Treasury
of
Mouse Stories
by
Beatrix Potter

This Book Belongs to:

_____

_____

A
Treasury
of
Mouse Stories
by
Beatrix Potter

With Illustrations by BEATRIX POTTER

DERRYDALE BOOKS
NEW YORK • AVENEL

This edition is published by Derrydale Books,
distributed by
Random House Value Publishing, Inc.
40 Engelhard Avenue, Avenel, New Jersey 07001.

Printed and bound in the United States of America

Library of Congress Cataloging-in-Publication Data

Potter, Beatrix, 1866–1943.
A treasury of mouse stories: the tales of Johnny Town-mouse and other mice /
by Beatrix Potter.
p. cm.
Summary: A collection of mouse stories including "The Tale of Two Bad Mice," "The Tailor of
Gloucester," "The Story of Miss Moppet," and others.
ISBN 0–517–12261–8
1. Children's stories, English. 2. Mice—Juvenile fiction.
[1. Mice—Fiction. 2. Short stories.] I. Title.
PZ7.P85Tp 1994
[E]—dc20   94-35476
CIP
AC

For this edition of *A Treasury of Mouse Stories by Beatrix Potter*
Cover design: Mary Helen Fink
Interior design: Melissa Ring
Production supervision: Roméo Enriquez
Editorial supervision: Claire Booss and Nina Rosenstein

8 7 6 5 4 3 2 1

Note: *This volume, with the exception of "The Tailor of Gloucester"—which has been edited—contains the complete and unabridged texts of the original stories, which have all been completely reset.*

CONTENTS

FOREWORD

Beatrix Potter understood mice. As with many youngsters who are powerfully shy with other people, young Beatrix's best friends were her mice and other small pets. When the cook trapped a mouse in the kitchen, Beatrix would rescue it and tame it. One of her first pets, her dormouse Xarifa, was, she later wrote, "in many respects the sweetest little animal I ever knew." Even as an adult, Potter would go to visit one of her few friends with a mouse, a rabbit, or another furry creature tucked into a little basket.

In *The Tale of Johnny Town-Mouse*, based on a well-known fable, Beatrix Potter's little country mouse unwittingly ends up in the city. After two hair-raising weeks of urban terrors, Timmy Willie returns home to his familiar, peaceful garden. When Johnny Town-mouse goes to visit his new friend in the country, he pines for the noise and excitement of the city. As for Beatrix Potter herself, "I prefer to live in the country, like Timmy Willie," she wrote.

That's not at all surprising. For Potter, the city of London—her "unloved birthplace," as she later called it—was the third-floor nursery where she spent most of her lonely childhood. She rarely left the nursery, never attended school (governesses came to teach her at home), and she had no childhood playmates other than her brother, Bertram, who was six years younger. Young Beatrix's opportunities for fun and freedom came during family vacations in Scotland, where she and Bertram could explore the countryside and discover flowers, butterflies, birds, and animals. Beatrix, who had already shown a talent for drawing and painting, spent many summer hours studying and copying fascinating details of nature. She and Bertram collected an assortment of little creatures—mice, rabbits, a tortoise, a hedgehog, and even bats.

Beatrix Potter never set out to be a writer of children's stories. Her first published book, *The Tale of Peter Rabbit*, was originally written as an illustrated letter to cheer up the sick child of her former governess Annie Moore, who had become a dear friend. Another story, written for another Moore child, became Potter's second—and favorite—published book, *The Tailor of Gloucester*. This was based on a real story, except that Beatrix Potter's version is peopled with little mice. No one knew better than she how to give these little creatures human personalities.

After Potter's unexpected success with her first published books, she excitedly began to plan more. She made each drawing after carefully observing living models and the details of life around her. "I can't invent: I can only copy," she once wrote. Every illustration in Potter's stories is a serious, comical, or satirical portrait of real life as she saw it. To draw the pictures for *The Tailor of Gloucester*, she needed to study a real tailor, so she popped a button off her jacket and sketched the tailor's cluttered studio while he worked. When Potter and her editor, Norman Warne, came up with the idea for *The Tale of Two Bad Mice*, Warne built a special little house with a glass back so that Potter could better observe her pet mice for the illustrations.

Potter's mice can be playful and rascally, while at other times industrious, kind, fearful, or brave. In *Ginger and Pickles*, the mice are minor characters: shop customers who are treated well by Pickles the dog and Ginger the cat because they realize that "it would never do to eat our own customers." In other stories, the mice are the main characters: A sassy little mouse outsmarts the cat that is teasing him in *The Story of Miss Moppet*. A fastidious mouse housekeeper is bothered by an assortment of messy visitors in *The Tale of Mrs. Tittlemouse*.

In *The Roly-Poly Pudding*, it is rats, not mice, that take center stage—and there's quite a difference between these related creatures! For Potter, the rats are the villains of the rodent family. When she bought her first farm, Hill Top, the house was infested with rats. Still, despite her dislike of the troublesome creatures, she grew to appreciate the antics of one particularly persistent and clever white rat, whom she named Mr. Samuel Whiskers. Mr. Whiskers is the featured villain in this story in which Tom Kitten notices a smell that is "something like mouse, only dreadfully strong," and soon finds himself in quite a mess.

After a little more than ten years, Beatrix Potter ended her publishing career and settled contentedly into the private life of a country farmer (in fact, if you peek down the lane in the illustration on page 57 you will see that Beatrix Potter has drawn herself into this little tale, along with many of the details of her beloved farmhouse and country neighborhood).

In this delightful treasury of Beatrix Potter's mice tales, we too can experience life in both the city and the country. Like Johnny Townmouse and Timmy Willie, we can weigh the differences between Beatrix Potter's own two worlds as we join in the adventures of these mischievous little creatures of the cupboards and the countryside.

NINA ROSENSTEIN

Westfield, New Jersey
1994

THE TALE OF
JOHNNY TOWN-MOUSE

To Aesop in the Shadows

Johnny Town-mouse was born in a cupboard. Timmy Willie was born in a garden. Timmy Willie was a little country mouse who went to town by mistake in a hamper. The gardener sent vegetables to town once a week by carrier; he packed them in a big hamper.

The gardener left the hamper by the garden gate, so that the carrier could pick it up when he passed. Timmy Willie crept in through a hole in the wickerwork, and after eating some peas—Timmy Willie fell fast asleep.

He awoke in a fright, while the hamper was being lifted into the carrier's cart. Then there was a jolting, and a clattering of horse's feet; other packages were thrown in; for miles and miles—jolt—jolt—jolt! and Timmy Willie trembled amongst the jumbled-up vegetables.

At last the cart stopped at a house, where the hamper was taken out, carried in, and set down. The cook gave the carrier sixpence; the back door banged, and the cart rumbled away. But there was no quiet; there seemed to be hundreds of carts passing. Dogs barked; boys whistled in the street; the cook laughed, the parlor maid ran up and down-stairs; and a canary sang like a steam engine.

Timmy Willie, who had lived all his life in a garden, was almost frightened to death. Presently the cook opened the hamper and began to unpack the vegetables. Out sprang the terrified Timmy Willie.

Up jumped the cook on a chair, exclaiming "A mouse! A mouse! Call the cat! Fetch me the poker, Sarah!" Timmy Willie did not wait for Sarah with the poker; he rushed along the skirting board till he came to a little hole, and in he popped.

He dropped half a foot, and crashed into the middle of a mouse dinner party, breaking three glasses—"Who in the world is this?" inquired Johnny Town-mouse. But after the first exclamation of surprise he instantly recovered his manners.

With the utmost politeness he introduced Timmy Willie to nine other mice, all with long tails and white neckties. Timmy Willie's own tail was insignificant. Johnny Town-mouse and his friends noticed it; but they were too well bred to make personal remarks; only one of them asked Timmy Willie if he had ever been in a trap?

The dinner was of eight courses; not much of anything, but truly elegant. All the dishes were unknown to Timmy Willie, who would have been a little afraid of tasting them; only he was very hungry, and very anxious to behave with company manners. The continual noise upstairs made him so nervous that he dropped a plate. "Never mind, they don't belong to us," said Johnny.

"Why don't those youngsters come back with the dessert?" It should be explained that two young mice, who were waiting on the others, went skirmishing upstairs to the kitchen between courses. Several times they had come tumbling in, squeaking and laughing; Timmy Willie learnt with horror that they were being chased by the cat. His appetite failed, he felt faint. "Try some jelly?" said Johnny Town-mouse.

"No? Would you rather go to bed? I will show you a most comfortable sofa pillow."

The sofa pillow had a hole in it. Johnny Town-mouse quite honestly recommended it as the best bed, kept exclusively for visitors. But the sofa smelt of cat. Timmy Willie preferred to spend a miserable night under the fender.

It was just the same the next day. An excellent breakfast was provided— for mice accustomed to eat bacon; but Timmy Willie had been reared on roots and salad. Johnny Town-mouse and his friends racketed about under the floors, and came boldly out all over the house in the evening. One particularly loud crash had been caused by Sarah tumbling downstairs with the tea tray; there were crumbs and sugar and smears of jam to be collected, in spite of the cat.

Timmy Willie longed to be at home in his peaceful nest in a sunny bank. The food disagreed with him; the noise prevented him from sleeping. In a few days he grew so thin that Johnny Town-mouse noticed it, and questioned him. He listened to Timmy Willie's story and inquired about the garden. "It sounds rather a dull place? What do you do when it rains?"

"When it rains, I sit in my little sandy burrow and shell corn and seeds from my Autumn store. I peep out at the throstles and blackbirds on the lawn, and my friend Cock Robin. And when the sun comes out again, you should see my garden and the flowers—roses and pinks and pansies— no noise except the birds and bees, and the lambs in the meadows."

"There goes that cat again!" exclaimed Johnny Town-mouse. When they had taken refuge in the coal cellar he resumed the conversation: "I confess I am a little disappointed; we have endeavored to entertain you, Timothy William."

"Oh yes, yes, you have been most kind; but I do feel so ill," said Timmy Willie.

"It may be that your teeth and digestion are unaccustomed to our food; perhaps it might be wiser for you to return in the hamper."

"Oh? Oh!" cried Timmy Willie.

"Why, of course, for the matter of that we could have sent you back last week," said Johnny rather huffily— "Did you not know that the hamper goes back empty on Saturdays?"

So Timmy Willie said good-bye to his new friends, and hid in the hamper with a crumb of cake and a withered cabbage leaf; and after much jolting, he was set down safely in his own garden.

Sometimes on Saturdays he went to look at the hamper lying by the gate, but he knew better than to get in again. And nobody got out, though Johnny Town-mouse had half promised a visit.

The winter passed; the sun came out again; Timmy Willie sat by his burrow warming his little fur coat and sniffing the smell of violets and spring grass. He had nearly forgotten his visit to town. When up the sandy path all spick and span with a brown leather bag came Johnny Town-mouse!

Timmy Willie received him with open arms. "You have come at the best of all the year; we will have herb pudding and sit in the sun."

"H'm'm! It is a little damp," said Johnny Town-mouse, who was carrying his tail under his arm, out of the mud.

"What is that fearful noise?" he started violently.

"That?" said Timmy Willie. "That is only a cow. I will beg a little milk; they are quite harmless, unless they happen to lie down upon you. How are all our friends?"

Johnny's account was rather middling. He explained why he was paying his visit so early in the season; the family had gone to the seaside for Easter; the cook was doing spring cleaning, on board wages, with particular instructions to clear out the mice. There were four kittens, and the cat had killed the canary.

"They say we did it, but I know better," said Johnny Town-mouse. "Whatever is that fearful racket?"

"That is only the lawnmower; I will fetch some of the grass clippings presently to make your bed. I am sure you had better settle in the country, Johnny."

"H'm'm—we shall see by Tuesday week; the hamper is stopped while they are at the seaside."

"I am sure you will never want to live in town again," said Timmy Willie.

But he did. He went back in the very next hamper of vegetables; he said it was too quiet!!

One place suits one person, another place suits another person. For my part, I prefer to live in the country, like Timmy Willie.

THE TAILOR OF GLOUCESTER

"I'll be at charges for a looking-glass;
And entertain a score or two of tailors."

Richard III

My Dear Freda:

Because you are fond of fairytales, and have been ill, I have made you a story all for yourself—a new one that nobody has read before.

And the queerest thing about it is—that I heard it in Gloucestershire, and that it is true—at least about the tailor, the waistcoat, and the

"No more twist!"

Christmas

In the time of swords and periwigs and full-skirted coats with flowered lappets—when gentlemen wore ruffles, and gold-laced waistcoats of paduasoy and taffeta—there lived a tailor in Gloucester.

He sat in the window of a little shop in Westgate Street, cross-legged on a table from morning till dark.

All day long while the light lasted he sewed and snippetted, piecing out his satin, and pompadour, and lutestring; stuffs had strange names, and were very expensive in the days of the Tailor of Gloucester.

But although he sewed fine silk for his neighbours, he himself was very, very poor. He cut his coats without waste; according to his embroidered cloth, they were very small ends and snippets that lay about upon the table—"Too narrow breadths for nought—except waistcoats for mice," said the tailor.

One bitter cold day near Christmastime the tailor began to make a coat (a coat of cherry-coloured corded silk embroidered with pansies and roses) and a cream-coloured satin waistcoat for the Mayor of Gloucester.

The tailor worked and worked, and he talked to himself: "No breadth at all, and cut on the cross; it is no breadth at all; tippets for mice and ribbons for mobs! for mice!" said the Tailor of Gloucester.

When the snow-flakes came down against the small leaded window-panes and shut out the light, the tailor had done his day's work; all the silk and satin lay cut out upon the table.

There were twelve pieces for the coat and four pieces for the waistcoat; and there were pocket-flaps and cuffs and buttons, all in order. For the lining of the coat there was fine yellow taffeta, and for the button-holes of the waistcoat there was cherry-coloured twist. And everything was ready to sew together in the morning, all measured and sufficient—except that there was wanting just one single skein of cherry-coloured twisted silk.

The tailor came out of his shop at dark. No one lived there at nights but little brown mice, and *they* ran in and out without any keys!

For behind the wooden wainscots of all the old houses in Gloucester, there are little mouse staircases and secret trap-doors; and the mice run from house to house through those long, narrow passages.

But the tailor came out of his shop and shuffled home through the snow. And although it was not a big house, the tailor was so poor he only rented the kitchen.

He lived alone with his cat; it was called Simpkin.

"Miaw?" said the cat when the tailor opened the door, "miaw?"

The tailor replied: "Simpkin, we shall make our fortune, but I am worn to a ravelling. Take this groat (which is our last fourpence), and, Simpkin, take a china pipkin, but a penn'orth of bread, a penn'orth of milk, and a penn'orth of sausages. And oh, Simpkin, with the last penny of our fourpence but me one penn'orth of cherry-coloured silk. But do not lose the last penny of the fourpence, Simpkin, or I am undone and worn to a thread-paper, for I have NO MORE TWIST."

Then Simpkin again said "Miaw!" and took the groat and the pipkin, and went out into the dark.

The tailor was very tired and beginning to be ill. He sat down by the hearth and talked to himself about that wonderful coat.

"I shall make my fortune—to be cut bias—the Mayor of Gloucester is to be married on Christmas Day in the morning, and he hath ordered a coat and an embroidered waistcoat—"

Then the tailor started; for suddenly, interrupting him, from the dresser at the other side of the kitchen came a number of little noises—

Tip tap, tip tap, tip tap tip!

"Now what can that be?" said the Tailor of Gloucester, jumping up from his chair. The tailor crossed the kitchen, and stood quite still beside the dresser, listening, and peering through his spectacles.

"This is very peculiar," said the Tailor of Gloucester, and he lifted up the tea-cup which was upside down.

Out stepped a little live lady mouse, and made a courtesy to the tailor! Then she hopped away down off the dresser, and under the wainscot.

The tailor sat down again by the fire, warming his poor cold hands. But all at once, from the dresser, there came other little noises—

Tip tap, tip tap, tip tap tip!

"This is passing extraordinary!" said the Tailor of Gloucester, and turned over another tea-cup, which was upside down.

Out stepped a little gentleman mouse, and made a bow to the tailor!

And out from under tea-cups and from under bowls and basins, stepped other and more little mice, who hopped away down off the dresser and under the wainscot.

The tailor sat down, close over the fire, lamenting: "One-and-twenty buttonholes of cherry-coloured silk! To be finished by noon of Saturday: and this is Tuesday evening. Was it right to let loose those mice, undoubtedly the property of Simpkin? Alack, I am undone, for I have no more twist!"

The little mice came out again and listened to the tailor; they took notice of the pattern of that wonderful coat. They whispered to one another about the taffeta lining and about little mouse tippets.

And then suddenly they all ran away together down the passage behind the wainscot, squeaking and calling to one another as they ran from house to house.

Not one mouse was left in the tailor's kitchen when Simpkin came back. He set down the pipkin of milk upon the dresser, and looked suspiciously at the tea-cups. He wanted his supper of little fat mouse!

"Simpkin," said the tailor, "where is my TWIST?"

But Simpkin hid a little parcel privately in the tea-pot, and spit and growled at the tailor; and if Simpkin had been able to talk, he would have asked: "Where is my MOUSE?"

"Alack, I am undone!" said the Tailor of Gloucester, and went sadly to bed.

All that night long Simpkin hunted and searched through the kitchen, peeping into cupboards and under the wainscot, and into the tea-pot where he had hidden that twist; but still he found never a mouse!

The poor old tailor was very ill with a fever, tossing and turning in his four-post bed; and still in his dreams he mumbled: "No more twist! no more twist!"

What should become of the cherry-coloured coat? Who should come to sew it, when the window was barred, and the door was fast locked?

Out-of-doors the market folks went trudging through the snow to buy their geese and turkeys, and to bake their Christmas pies; but there would be no dinner for Simpkin and the poor old tailor of Gloucester.

The tailor lay ill for three days and nights; and then it was Christmas Eve, and very late at night. And still Simpkin wanted his mice, and mewed as he stood beside the four-post bed.

But it is in the old story that all the beasts can talk in the night between Christmas Eve and Christmas Day in the morning (though there are very few folk that can hear them, or know what it is that they say).

When the Cathedral clock struck twelve there was an answer—like an echo of the chimes—and Simpkin heard it, and came out of the tailor's door, and wandered about in the snow.

From all the roofs and gables and old wooden houses in Gloucester came a thousand merry voices singing the old Christmas rhymes—all the old songs that ever I heard of, and some that I don't know, like Whittington's bells.

Under the wooden eaves the starlings and sparrows sang of Christmas pies; the jackdaws woke up in the Cathedral tower; and although it was the middle of the night the throstles and robins sang; and air was quite full of little twittering tunes.

But it was all rather provoking to poor hungry Simpkin.

From the tailor's ship in Westgate came a glow of light; and when Simpkin crept up to peep in at the window it was full of candles. There was a snippeting of scissors, and snappeting of thread; and little mouse voices sang loudly and gaily:

"Four-and-twenty tailors
Went to catch a snail,
The best man amongst them
Durst not touch her tail;
She put out her horns
Like a little kyloe cow.
Run, tailors, run!
Or she'll have you all e'en now!"

Then without a pause the little mouse voices went on again:

"Sieve my lady's oatmeal,
Grind my lady's flour,
Put it in a chestnut,
Let it stand an hour—"

"Mew! Mew!" interrupted Simpkin, and he scratched at the door. But the key was under the tailor's pillow; he could not get in.

The little mice only laughed, and tried another tune—

"Three little mice sat down to spin,
Pussy passed by and she peeped in.
What are you at, my fine little men?
Making coats for gentlemen.
Shall I come in and cut off yours threads?
Oh, no, Miss Pussy,
You'd bite off our heads!"

"Mew! scratch! scratch!" scuffled Simpkin on the window-sill; while the little mice inside sprang to their feet, and all began to shout all at once in little twittering voices: "No more twist! No more twist!" And they barred up the window-shutters and shut out Simpkin.

Simpkin came away from the shop and went home considering in his mind. He found the poor old tailor without fever, sleeping peacefully.

Then Simpkin went on tip-toe and took a little parcel of silk out of the tea-pot; and looked at it in the moonlight; and he felt quite ashamed of his badness compared with those good little mice!

When the tailor awoke in the morning, the first thing which he saw, upon the patchwork quilt, was a skein of cherry-coloured twisted silk, and beside his bed stood the repentant Simpkin!

The sun was shining on the snow when the tailor got up and dressed, and came out into the street with Simpkin running before him.

"Alack," said the tailor, "I have my twist; but no more strength—nor time—than will serve to make me one single buttonhole; for this is Christmas Day in the Morning! The Mayor of Gloucester shall be married by noon—and where is his cherry-coloured coat?"

He unlocked the door of the little shop in Westgate Street, and Simpkin ran in, like a cat that expects something.

But there was no one there! Not even one little brown mouse!

But upon the table—oh joy! the tailor gave a shout—there, where he had left plain cuttings of silk—there lay the most beautiful coat and embroidered satin waistcoat that ever were worn by a Mayor of Gloucester!

Everything was finished except just one single cherry-coloured buttonhole, and where that buttonhole was wanting there was pinned a scrap of paper with these words—in little teeny weeny writing—

NO MORE TWIST.

And from then began the luck of the Tailor of Gloucester; he grew quite stout, and he grew quite rich.

He made the most wonderful waistcoats for all the rich merchants of Gloucester, and for all the fine gentlemen of the country round.

Never were seen such ruffles, or such embroidered cuffs and lappets! But his buttonholes were the greatest triumph of it all.

The stitches of those buttonholes were so neat—*so* neat—I wonder how they could be stitched by an old man in spectacles, with crooked old fingers, and a tailor's thimble.

The stitches of those buttonholes were so small—*so* small—they looked as if they had been made by little mice!

THE TALE OF
TWO BAD MICE

For W.M.L.W., the Little Girl
Who Had the Doll's House

Once upon a time there was a very beautiful doll's-house; it was red brick with white windows, and it had real muslin curtains and a front door and a chimney.

It belonged to two Dolls called Lucinda and Jane; at least it belonged to Lucinda, but she never ordered meals.

Jane was the Cook; but she never did any cooking, because the dinner had been bought ready-made, in a box full of shavings.

There were two red lobsters and a ham, a fish, a pudding, and some pears and oranges.

They would not come off the plates, but they were extremely beautiful.

One morning Lucinda and Jane had gone out for a drive in the doll's perambulator. There was no one in the nursery, and it was very quiet. Presently there was a little scuffling, scratching noise in a corner near the fireplace, where there was a hole under the skirting-board.

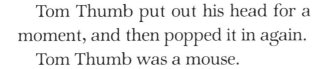

Tom Thumb put out his head for a moment, and then popped it in again. Tom Thumb was a mouse.

A minute afterwards, Hunca Munca, his wife, put her head out, too; and when she saw that there was no one in the nursery, she ventured out on the oilcloth under the coal-box.

The doll's-house stood at the other side of the fire-place. Tom Thumb and Hunca Munca went cautiously across the hearthrug. They pushed the front door—it was not fast.

Tom Thumb and Hunca Munca went upstairs and peeped into the dining-room. Then they squeaked with joy!

Such a lovely dinner was laid out upon the table! There were tin spoons, and lead knives and forks, and two dolly-chairs—all *so* convenient!

Tom Thumb set to work at once to carve the ham. It was a beautiful shiny yellow, streaked with red.

The knife crumpled up and hurt him; he put his finger in his mouth.

"It is not boiled enough; it is hard. You have a try, Hunca Munca."

Hunca Munca stood up in her chair, and chopped at the ham with another lead knife.

"It's as hard as the hams at the cheesemonger's," said Hunca Munca.

The ham broke off the plate with a jerk, and rolled under the table.

"Let it alone," said Tom Thumb; "give me some fish, Hunca Munca!"

Hunca Munca tried every tin spoon in turn; the fish was glued to the dish.

Then Tom Thumb lost his temper. He put the ham in the middle of the floor, and hit it with the tongs and with the shovel—bang, bang, smash, smash!

The ham flew all into pieces, for underneath the shiny paint it was made of nothing but plaster!

Then there was no end to the rage and disappointment of Tom Thumb and Hunca Munca. They broke up the pudding, the lobsters, the pears and the oranges.

As the fish would not come off the plate, they put it into the red-hot crinkly paper fire in the kitchen; but it would not burn either.

Tom Thumb went up the kitchen chimney and looked out at the top—there was no soot.

While Tom Thumb was up the chimney, Hunca Munca had another disappointment. She found some tiny canisters upon the dresser, labelled—

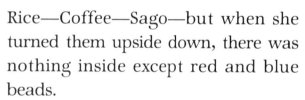

Rice—Coffee—Sago—but when she turned them upside down, there was nothing inside except red and blue beads.

Then those mice set to work to do all the mischief they could—especially Tom Thumb! He took Jane's clothes out of the chest of drawers in her bedroom, and he threw them out of the top floor window.

But Hunca Munca had a frugal mind. After pulling half the feathers out of Lucinda's bolster, she remembered that she herself was in want of a feather bed.

With Tom Thumbs's assistance she carried the bolster downstairs, and across the hearth-rug. It was difficult to squeeze the bolster into the mouse-hole; but they managed it somehow.

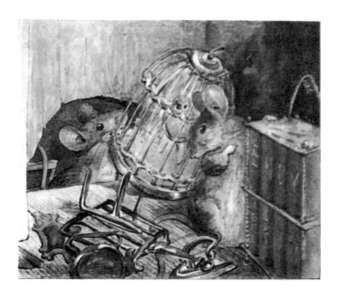

Then Hunca Munca went back and fetched a chair, a book-case, a bird-cage, and several small odds and ends. The book-case and the bird-cage refused to go into the mousehole.

Hunca Munca left them behind the coal-box, and went to fetch a cradle.

Hunca Munca was just returning with another chair, when suddenly there was a noise of talking outside upon the landing. The mice rushed back to their hole, and the dolls came into the nursery.

What a sight met the eyes of Jane and Lucinda! Lucinda sat upon the upset kitchen stove and stared; and Jane leant against the kitchen dresser and smiled—but neither of them made any remark.

The book-case and the bird-cage were rescued from under the coal-box—but Hunca Munca has got the cradle, and some of Lucinda's clothes.

She also has some useful pots and pans, and several other things.

The little girl that the doll's-house belonged to, said,—"I will get a doll dressed like a policeman!"

But the nurse said,—"I will set a mouse-trap!"

So that is the story of the two Bad Mice,—but they were not so very very naughty after all, because Tom Thumb paid for everything he broke.

He found a crooked sixpence under the hearth-rug; and upon Christmas Eve, he and Hunca Munca stuffed it into one of the stockings of Lucinda and Jane.

And very early every morning— before anybody is awake—Hunca Munca comes with her dust-pan and her broom to sweep the Dollies' house!

THE STORY OF
MISS MOPPET

This is a Pussy called Miss Moppet; she thinks she has heard a mouse!

This is the Mouse peeping out behind the cupboard and making fun of Miss Moppet. He is not afraid of a kitten.

This is Miss Moppet jumping just too late; she misses the Mouse and hits her own head.

She thinks it is a very hard cupboard!

The Mouse watches Miss Moppet from the top of the cupboard.

Miss Moppet ties up her head in a duster and sits before the fire.

The Mouse thinks she is looking very ill. He comes sliding down the bellpull.

Miss Moppet looks worse and worse. The Mouse comes a little nearer.

Miss Moppet holds her poor head in her paws and looks at him through a hole in the duster. The Mouse comes *very* close.

And then all of a sudden—Miss Moppet jumps upon the Mouse!

And because the Mouse has teased Miss Moppet—Miss Moppet thinks she will tease the Mouse, which is not at all nice of Miss Moppet.

She ties him up in the duster and tosses it about like a ball.

But she forgot about that hole in the duster; and when she untied it—there was no Mouse!

He has wriggled out and run away; and he is dancing a jig on top of the cupboard!

THE
ROLY-POLY PUDDING

In Remembrance of "Sammy,"
the Intelligent Pink-Eyed Representative of
a Persecuted (But Irrepressible) Race.
An Affectionate Little Friend,
and Most Accomplished Thief!

Once upon a time there was an old cat, called Mrs. Tabitha Twitchit, who was an anxious parent. She used to lose her kittens continually, and whenever they were lost they were always in mischief!

On baking day she determined to shut them up in a cupboard.

She caught Moppet and Mittens, but she could not find Tom.

Mrs. Tabitha went up and down all over the house, mewing for Tom Kitten. She looked in the pantry under the staircase, and she searched the best spare bedroom that was all covered up with dust sheets. She went right upstairs and looked into the attics, but she could not find him anywhere.

It was an old, old house, full of cupboards and passages. Some of the walls were four feet thick, and there used to be queer noises inside them, as if there might be a little secret staircase. Certainly there were odd little jagged doorways in the wainscot, and things disappeared at night— especially cheese and bacon.

Mrs. Tabitha became more and more distracted and mewed dreadfully.

While their mother was searching the house, Moppet and Mittens had got into mischief.

The cupboard door was not locked, so they pushed it open and came out.

They went straight to the dough which was set to rise in a pan before the fire.

They patted it with their little soft paws—"Shall we make dear little muffins?" said Mittens to Moppet.

But just at that moment somebody knocked at the front door, and Moppet jumped into the flour barrel in a fright.

Mittens ran away to the dairy and hid in an empty jar on the stone shelf where the milk pans stand.

The visitor was a neighbor, Mrs. Ribby; she had called to borrow some yeast.

Mr. Tabitha came downstairs mewing dreadfully—"Come in, Cousin Ribby, come in, and sit ye down! I'm in sad trouble, Cousin Ribby," said Tabitha, shedding tears. "I've lost my dear son Thomas; I'm afraid the rats have got him." She wiped her eyes with her apron.

"He's a bad kitten, Cousin Tabitha; he made a cat's cradle of my best bonnet last time I came to tea. Where have you looked for him?"

"All over the house! The rats are too many for me. What a thing it is to have an unruly family!" said Mrs. Tabitha Twitchit.

"I'm not afraid of rats; I will help you to find him; and whip him, too! What is all that soot in the fender?"

"The chimney wants sweeping— Oh, dear me, Cousin Ribby—now Moppet and Mittens are gone!

"They have both got out of the cupboard!"

Ribby and Tabitha set to work to search the house thoroughly again. They poked under the beds with Ribby's umbrella and they rummaged in cupboards. They even fetched a candle and looked inside a clothes chest in one of the attics. They could not find anything, but once they heard a door bang and somebody scuttered downstairs.

"Yes, it is infested with rats," said Tabitha tearfully. "I caught seven young ones out of one hole in the back kitchen, and we had them for dinner last Saturday. And once I saw the old father rat—an enormous old rat— Cousin Ribby. I was just going to jump upon him, when he showed his yellow teeth at me and whisked down the hole.

"The rats get upon my nerves, Cousin Ribby," said Tabitha.

Ribby and Tabitha searched and searched. They both heard a curious roly-poly noise under the attic floor. But there was nothing to be seen.

They returned to the kitchen. "Here's one of your kittens at least," said Ribby, dragging Moppet out of the flour barrel.

They shook the flour off her and set her down on the kitchen floor. She seemed to be in a terrible fright.

"Oh! Mother, Mother," said Moppet, "there's been an old woman rat in the kitchen, and she's stolen some of the dough!"

The two cats ran to look at the dough pan. Sure enough there were marks of little scratching fingers, and a lump of dough was gone!

"Which way did she go, Moppet?"

But Moppet had been too much frightened to peep out of the barrel again.

Ribby and Tabitha took her with them to keep her safely in sight, while they went on with their search.

They went into the dairy.
The first thing they found was Mittens, hiding in an empty jar.

They tipped over the jar, and she scrambled out.

"Oh, Mother, Mother!" said Mittens—

"Oh! Mother, Mother, there has been an old man rat in the dairy—a dreadful 'normous big rat, Mother; and he's stolen a pat of butter and the rolling pin."

Ribby and Tabitha looked at one another.

"A rolling pin and butter! Oh, my poor son Thomas!" exclaimed Tabitha, wringing her paws.

"A rolling pin?" said Ribby. "Did we not hear a roly-poly noise in the attic when we were looking into that chest?"

Ribby and Tabitha rushed upstairs again. Sure enough the roly-poly noise was still going on quite distinctly under the attic floor.

"This is serious, Cousin Tabitha," said Ribby. "We must send for John Joiner at once, with a saw."

Now, this is what had been happening to Tom Kitten, and it shows how very unwise it is to go up a chimney in a very old house, where a person does not know his way, and where there are enormous rats.

Tom Kitten did not want to be shut up in a cupboard. When he saw that his mother was going to bake, he determined to hide.

He looked about for a nice convenient place, and he fixed upon the chimney.

The fire had only just been lighted, and it was not hot; but there was a white choky smoke from the green sticks. Tom Kitten got upon the fender and looked up. It was a big old-fashioned fireplace.

The chimney itself was wide enough inside for a man to stand up and walk about. So there was plenty of room for a little Tom Cat.

He jumped right up into the fireplace, balancing himself upon the iron bar where the kettle hangs.

Tom Kitten took another big jump off the bar and landed on a ledge high up inside the chimney, knocking down some soot into the fender.

Tom Kitten coughed and choked with the smoke; he could hear the sticks beginning to crackle and burn in the fireplace down below. He made up his mind to climb right to the top, and get out on the slates, and try to catch sparrows.

"I cannot go back. If I slipped I might fall in the fire and singe my beautiful tail and my little blue jacket."

The chimney was a very big old-fashioned one. It was built in the days when people burnt logs of wood upon the hearth.

The chimney stack stood up above the roof like a little stone tower, and the daylight shone down from the top, under the slanting slates that kept out the rain.

Tom Kitten was getting very frightened! He climbed up, and up, and up.

Then he waded sideways through inches of soot. He was like a little sweep himself.

It was most confusing in the dark. One flue seemed to lead into another.

There was less smoke, but Tom Kitten felt quite lost.

He scrambled up and up; but before he reached the chimney top he came to a place where somebody had loosened a stone in the wall. There were some mutton bones lying about.

"This seems funny," said Tom Kitten. "Who has been gnawing bones up here in the chimney? I wish I had never come! And what a funny smell? It is something like mouse, only dreadfully strong. It makes me sneeze," said Tom Kitten.

He squeezed through the hole in the wall and dragged himself along a most uncomfortably tight passage where there was scarcely any light.

He groped his way carefully for several yards; he was at the back of the skirting board in the attic, where there is a little mark * in the picture.

All at once he fell head over heels in the dark, down a hole, and landed on a heap of very dirty rags.

When Tom Kitten picked himself up and looked about him, he found himself in a place that he had never seen before, although he had lived all his life in the house. It was a very small stuffy fusty room, with boards, and rafters, and cobwebs, and lath and plaster.

Opposite to him—as far away as he could sit—was an enormous rat.

"What do you mean by tumbling into my bed all covered with smuts?" said the rat, chattering his teeth.

"Please, sir, the chimney wants sweeping," said poor Tom Kitten.

"Anna Maria! Anna Maria!" squeaked the rat. There was a pattering noise and an old woman rat poked her head round a rafter.

All in a minute she rushed upon Tom Kitten, and before he knew what was happening...

...his coat was pulled off, and he was rolled up in a bundle, and tied with string in very hard knots.

Anna Maria did the tying. The old rat watched her and took snuff. When she had finished, they both sat staring at him with their mouths open.

"Anna Maria," said the old man rat (whose name was Samuel Whiskers), "Anna Maria, make me a kitten dumpling roly-poly pudding for my dinner."

"It requires dough and a pat of butter and a rolling pin," said Anna Maria, considering Tom Kitten with her head on one side.

"No," said Samuel Whiskers, "make it properly, Anna Maria, with breadcrumbs."

"Nonsense! Butter and dough," replied Anna Maria.

The two rats consulted together for a few minutes and then went away.

Samuel Whiskers got through a hole in the wainscot and went boldly down the front staircase to the dairy to get the butter. He did not meet anybody.

He made a second journey for the rolling pin. He pushed it in front of him with his paws, like a brewer's man trundling a barrel.

He could hear Ribby and Tabitha talking, but they were too busy lighting the candle to look into the chest.

They did not see him.

Anna Maria went down by way of skirting board and a window shutter to the kitchen to steal the dough.

She borrowed a small saucer and scooped up the dough with her paws.
She did not observe Moppet.

While Tom Kitten was left alone under the floor of the attic, he wriggled about and tried to mew for help.

But his mouth was full of soot and cobwebs, and he was tied up in such very tight knots, he could not make anybody hear him.

Except a spider who came out of a crack in the ceiling and examined the knots critically, from a safe distance.

It was a judge of knots because it had a habit of tying up unfortunate bluebottles. It did not offer to assist him.

Tom Kitten wriggled and squirmed until he was quite exhausted.

Presently the rats came back and set to work to make him into a dumpling. First they smeared him with butter, and then they rolled him in the dough.

"Will not the string be very indigestible, Anna Maria?" inquired Samuel Whiskers.

Anna Maria said she thought that it was of no consequence; but she wished that Tom Kitten would hold his head still, as it disarranged the pastry. She laid hold of his ears.

Tom Kitten bit and spit, and mewed and wriggled; and the rolling pin went roly-poly, roly; roly-poly, roly. The rats each held an end.

"His tail is sticking out! You did not fetch enough dough, Anna Maria."

"I fetched as much as I could carry," replied Anna Maria.

"I do not think"— said Samuel Whiskers, pausing to take a look at Tom Kitten—"I do *not* think it will be a good pudding. It smells sooty."

Anna Maria was about to argue the point when all at once there began to be other sounds up above—the rasping noise of a saw, and the noise of a little dog, scratching and yelping!

The rats dropped the rolling pin and listened attentively.

"We are discovered and interrupted, Anna Maria; let us collect our property—and other people's—and depart at once.

"I fear that we shall be obliged to leave this pudding.

"But I am persuaded that the knots would have proved indigestible, whatever you may urge to the contrary."

"Come away at once and help me to tie up some mutton bones in a counterpane," said Anna Maria. "I have got half a smoked ham hidden in the chimney."

So it happened that by the time John Joiner had got the plank up— there was nobody here under the floor except the rolling pin and Tom Kitten in a very dirty dumpling!

But there was a strong smell of rats; and John Joiner spent the rest of the morning sniffing and whining, and wagging his tail, and going round and round with his head in the hole like a gimlet.

Then he nailed the plank down again and put his tools in his bag, and came downstairs.

The cat family had quite recovered. They invited him to stay to dinner.

The dumpling had been peeled off Tom Kitten and made separately into a bag pudding, with currants in it to hide the smuts.

They had been obliged to put Tom Kitten into a hot bath to get the butter off.

John Joiner smelt the pudding; but he regretted that he had not time to stay to dinner, because he had just finished making a wheelbarrow for Miss Potter, and she had ordered two hen coops.

And when I was going to the post late in the afternoon—I looked up the land from the corner, and I saw Mr. Samuel Whiskers and his wife on the run, with big bundles on a little wheelbarrow, which looked very much like mine.

They were just turning in at the gate to the barn of Farmer Potatoes.

Samuel Whiskers was puffing and out of breath. Anna Maria was still arguing in shrill tones.

She seemed to know her way, and she seemed to have a quantity of luggage.

I am sure *I* never gave her leave to borrow my wheelbarrow!

They went into the barn and hauled their parcels with a bit of string to the top of the haymow.

After that, there were no more rats for a long time at Tabitha Twitchit's.

As for Farmer Potatoes, he has been driven nearly distracted. There are rats, and rats, and rats in his barn! They eat up the chicken food, and steal the oats and bran, and make holes in the meal bags.

And they are all descended from Mr. and Mrs. Samuel Whiskers—children and grandchildren and great-great-grandchildren.

There is no end to them!

Moppet and Mittens have grown up into very good rat-catchers.

They go out rat-catching in the village, and they find plenty of employment. They charge so much a dozen and earn their living very comfortably.

They hang up the rats' tails in a row on the barn door, to show how many they have caught—dozens and dozens of them.

But Tom Kitten has always been afraid of a rat; he never durst face anything that is bigger than—

A Mouse.

GINGER AND PICKLES

Dedicated
With very kind regards to old Mr. John Taylor,
Who "thinks he might pass as a dormouse,"
(Three years in bed and never a grumble!).

Once upon a time there was a village shop. The name over the window was "Ginger and Pickles."

It was a little small shop just the right size for Dolls—Lucinda and Jane Doll-cook always bought their groceries at Ginger and Pickles.

The counter inside was a convenient height for rabbits. Ginger and Pickles sold red spotty pocket handkerchiefs at a penny three farthings.

They also sold sugar, and snuff and galoshes.

In fact, although it was such a small shop it sold nearly everything—except a few things that you want in a hurry—like bootlaces, hairpins and mutton chops.

Ginger and Pickles were the people who kept the shop. Ginger was a yellow tomcat, and Pickles was a terrier.

The rabbits were always a little bit afraid of Pickles.

The shop was also patron-
ized by mice—only the mice
were rather afraid of Ginger.

Ginger usually requested
Pickles to serve them, because
he said it made his mouth
water.

"I cannot bear," said he, "to
see them going out at the door
carrying their little parcels."

"I have the same feeling
about rats," replied Pickles,
"but it would never do to eat
our customers; they would
leave us and go to Tabitha
Twitchit's."

"On the contrary, they
would go nowhere," replied
Ginger gloomily.

(Tabitha Twitchit kept the
only other shop in the village.
She did not give credit.)

Ginger and Pickles gave unlimited credit.

Now the meaning of "credit" is this—when a customer buys a bar of soap, instead of the customer pulling out a purse and paying for it —she says she will pay another time.

And Pickles makes a low bow and says, "With pleasure, madam," and it is written down in a book.

The customers come again and again, and buy quantities, in spite of being afraid of Ginger and Pickles.

But there is no money in what is called the "till."

The customers came in crowds every day and bought quantities, especially the toffee customers. But there was always no money; they never paid for as much as a pennyworth of peppermints.

But the sales were enormous, ten times as large as Tabitha Twitchit's.

As there was always no money, Ginger and Pickles were obliged to eat their own goods.

Pickles ate biscuits and Ginger ate a dried haddock.

They ate them by candlelight after the shop was closed.

When it came to Jan. 1st there was still no money, and Pickles was unable to buy a dog license.

"It is very unpleasant, I am afraid of the police," said Pickles.

"It is your own fault for being a terrier; *I* do not require a license, and neither does Kep, the Collie dog."

"It is very uncomfortable, I am afraid I shall be summoned. I have tried in vain to get a license upon credit at the Post Office;" said Pickles. "The place is full of policemen. I met one as I was coming home.

"Let us send in the bill again to Samuel Whiskers, Ginger, he owes 22/9 for bacon."

"I do not believe that he intends to pay at all," replied Ginger.

"And I feel sure that Anna Maria pockets things—

"Where are all the cream crackers?"

"You have eaten them yourself," replied Ginger.

Ginger and Pickles retired into the back parlor.

They did accounts. They added up sums and sums, and sums.

"Samuel Whiskers has run up a bill as long as his tail; he has had an ounce and three-quarters of snuff since October.

"What is seven pounds of butter at 1/3, and a stick of sealing wax and four matches?"

"Send in all the bills again to everybody 'with compliments,' " replied Ginger.

After a time they heard a noise in the shop, as if something had been pushed in at the door. They came out of the back parlor. There was an envelope lying on the counter, and a policeman writing in a notebook!

Pickles nearly had a fit, he barked and he barked and made little rushes.

"Bite him, Pickles! bite him!" spluttered Ginger behind a sugar barrel, "he's only a German doll!"

The policeman went on writing in his notebook; twice he put his pencil in his mouth, and once he dipped it in the treacle.

Pickles barked till he was hoarse. But still the policeman took no notice. He had bead eyes, and his helmet was sewed on with stitches.

At length on his last little rush—Pickles found that the shop was empty. The policeman had disappeared.

But the envelope remained.

"Do you think that he has gone to fetch a real live policeman? I am afraid it is a summons," said Pickles.

"No," replied Ginger, who had opened the envelope, "it is the rates and taxes, £3 19 11¾."

"This is the last straw," said Pickles, "let us close the shop."

They put up the shutters, and left. But they have not removed from the neighborhood. In fact some people wish they had gone further.

Ginger is living in the war-ren [game preserve for rab-bits]. I do not know what occupation he pursues; he looks stout and comfortable.

Pickles is at present a game-keeper.

The closing of the shop caused great inconvenience. Tabitha Twitchit immediately raised the price of everything a halfpenny; and she continued to refuse to give credit.

Of course there are the tradesmen's carts—the butcher, the fishman and Timothy Baker.

But a person cannot live on "seed wigs" and sponge cake and butter buns—not even when the sponge cake is as good as Timothy's!

After a time Mr. John Dormouse and his daughter began to sell peppermints and candles.

But they did not keep "self-fitting sixes"; and it takes five mice to carry one seven inch candle.

Besides—the candles which they sell behave very strangely in warm weather.

And Miss Dormouse refused to take back the ends when they were brought back to her with complaints.

And when Mr. John Dormouse was complained to, he stayed in bed, and would say nothing but "very snug;" which is not the way to carry on a retail business.

So everybody was pleased when Sally Henny Penny sent out a printed poster to say that she was going to reopen the shop—"Henny's Opening Sale! Grand cooperative Jumble! Penny's penny prices! Come buy, come try, come buy!"

The poster really was most 'ticing.

There was a rush upon the opening day. The shop was crammed with customers, and there were crowds of mice upon the biscuit cannisters.

Sally Henny Penny gets rather flustered when she tries to count out change, and she insists on being paid cash; but she is quite harmless.

And she has laid in a remarkable assortment of bargains.

There is something to please everybody.

THE TALE OF
MRS. TITTLEMOUSE

Nellie's
Little Book

Once upon a time there was a woodmouse, and her name was Mrs. Tittlemouse.

She lived in a bank under a hedge.

Such a funny house! There were yards and yards of sandy passages, leading to store-rooms and nut cellars and seed cellars, all amongst the roots of the hedge.

There was a kitchen, a parlor, a pantry, and a larder.

Also, there was Mrs. Tittlemouse's bedroom, where she slept in a little box bed!

Mrs. Tittlemouse was a most terribly tidy particular little mouse, always sweeping and dusting the soft sandy floors.

Sometimes a beetle lost its way in the passages.

"Shuh! shuh! little dirty feet!" said Mrs. Tittlemouse, clattering her dustpan.

And one day a little old woman ran up and down in a red spotty cloak.

"Your house is on fire, Mother Ladybird! Fly away home to your children!"

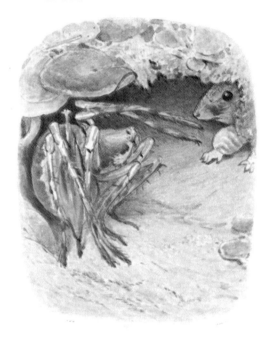

Another day, a big fat spider came in to shelter from the rain.

"Beg pardon, is this not Miss Muffet's?"

"Go away, you bold bad spider! Leaving ends of cobweb all over my nice clean house!"

She bundled the spider out at a window.

He let himself down the hedge with a long thin bit of string.

Mrs. Tittlemouse went on her way to a distant storeroom, to fetch cherrystones and thistle-down seed for dinner.

All along the passage she sniffed, and looked at the floor.

"I smell a smell of honey; is it the cowslips outside, in the hedge? I am sure I can see the marks of little dirty feet."

Suddenly round a corner, she met Babbitty Bumble—"Zizz, Bizz, Bizzz!" said the bumble bee.

Mrs. Tittlemouse looked at her severely. She wished that she had a broom.

"Good-day, Babbitty Bumble; I should be glad to buy some beeswax. But what are you doing down here? Why do you always come in at a window, and say, Zizz, Bizz, Bizzz?" Mrs. Tittlemouse began to get cross.

"Zizz, Wizz, Wizzz!" replied Babbitty Bumble in a peevish squeak. She sidled down a passage, and disappeared into a storeroom which had been used for acorns.

Mrs. Tittlemouse had eaten the acorns before Christmas; the storeroom ought to have been empty.

But it was full of untidy dry moss.

Mrs. Tittlemouse began to pull out the moss. Three or four other bees put their heads out, and buzzed fiercely.

"I am not in the habit of letting lodgings; this is an intrusion!" said Mrs. Tittlemouse. "I will have them turned out —" "Buzz! Buzz! Buzzz!"—"I wonder who would help me?" "Bizz, Wizz, Wizzz!"

—"I will not have Mr. Jackson; he never wipes his feet."

Mrs. Tittlemouse decided to leave the bees till after dinner.

When she got back to the parlor, she heard some one coughing in a fat voice; and there sat Mr. Jackson himself!

He was sitting all over a small rocking chair, twiddling his thumbs and smiling, with his feet on the fender.

He lived in a drain below the hedge, in a very dirty wet ditch.

"How do you do, Mr. Jackson? Deary me, you have got very wet!"

"Thank you, thank you, thank you, Mrs. Tittlemouse! I'll sit awhile and dry myself," said Mr. Jackson.

He sat and smiled, and the water dripped off his coat tails. Mrs. Tittlemouse went round with a mop.

He sat such a while that he had to be asked if he would take some dinner?

First she offered him cherry-stones. "Thank you, thank you, Mrs. Tittlemouse! No teeth, no teeth, no teeth!" said Mr. Jackson.

He opened his mouth most un-necessarily wide; he certainly had not a tooth in his head.

Then she offered him thistle-down seed—"Tiddly, widdly, widdly! Pouff, pouff, puff!" said Mr. Jackson. He blew the thistle-down all over the room.

"Thank you, thank you, thank you, Mrs. Tittlemouse! Now what I really—*really* should like—would be a little dish of honey!"

"I am afraid I have not got any, Mr. Jackson!" said Mrs. Tittlemouse.

"Tiddly, widdly, widdly, Mrs. Tittlemouse!" said the smiling Mr. Jackson, "I can *smell* it; that is why I came to call."

Mr. Jackson rose ponderously from the table, and began to look into the cupboards.

Mrs. Tittlemouse followed him with a dishcloth, to wipe his large wet footmarks off the parlor floor.

When he had convinced himself that there was no honey in the cupboards, he began to walk down the passage.

"Indeed, indeed, you will stick fast, Mr. Jackson!"

"Tiddly, widdly, widdly, Mrs. Tittlemouse!"

First he squeezed into the pantry.

"Tiddly, widdly, widdly? No honey? No honey, Mrs. Tittlemouse?"

There were three creepy-crawly people hiding in the plate rack. Two of them got away; but the littlest one he caught.

Then he squeezed into the larder. Miss Butterfly was tasting the sugar; but she flew away out of the window.

"Tiddly, widdly, widdly, Mrs. Tittlemouse; you seem to have plenty of visitors!"

"And without any invitation!" said Mrs. Thomasina Tittlemouse.

They went along the sandy passage—"Tiddly, widdly—" "Buzz! Wizz! Wizz!"

He met Babbitty round a corner, and snapped her up, and put her down again.

"I do not like bumble bees. They are all over bristles," said Mr. Jackson, wiping his mouth with his coat sleeve.

"Get out, you nasty old toad!" shrieked Babbitty Bumble.

"I shall go distracted!" scolded Mrs. Tittlemouse.

She shut herself up in the nut cellar while Mr. Jackson pulled out the bees-nest. He seemed to have no objection to stings.

When Mrs. Tittlemouse ventured to come out—everybody had gone away.

But the untidiness was something dreadful—"Never did I see such a mess—smears of honey; and moss, and thistledown—and marks of big and little dirty feet— all over my nice clean house!"

She gathered up the moss and the remains of the beeswax.

Then she went out and fetched some twigs, to partly close up the front door.

"I will make it too small for Mr. Jackson!"

She fetched soft soap, and flannel, and a new scrubbing brush from the storeroom. But she was too tired to do any more. First she fell asleep in her chair, and then she went to bed.

"Will it ever be tidy again?" said poor Mrs. Tittlemouse.

Next morning she got up very early and began a spring cleaning which lasted a fortnight.

She swept, and scrubbed, and dusted; and she rubbed up the furniture with beeswax, and polished her little tin spoons.

When it was all beautifully neat and clean, she gave a party to five other little mice, without Mr. Jackson.

He smelt the party and came up the bank, but he could not squeeze in at the door.

So they handed him out acorn cupfuls of honeydew through the window, and he was not at all offended.

He sat outside in the sun, and said—"Tiddly, widdly, widdly! Your very good health, Mrs. Tittlemouse!"